Praise for Dayle A. Dermatis

"…One of the best writers working today."

—*USA Today* bestselling author
Dean Wesley Smith

"Another awesome flash piece is, 'The Return' by Dayle A. Dermatis. This coming of age flash blends ancestor worship and lunar travel through a poetically inventive conceit of 'speaking trees'. This piece is a flash SF triumph, recommended for both theme and technique."

—sfreader.com

"I was particularly struck by the little gem, 'Sultan's Sons' by Dayle A. Dermatis. This was, in my opinion, the… strongest story in the entire collection."

—horrorreader.com

"You want something new and something fresh and I think I got that when I accepted ['The Sultan's Sons'] from…Dayle Dermatis."

—Armand Rosamilia, Editor of *Clash of Steel*

Also by Dayle A. Dermatis

Collections

Five Funny Fantasies

*Written on the Coast: Thirteen Tales of
Magic and Mayhem Written in Lincoln City, OR*

Short Stories

"Desperate Housewitches"
"Leave a Candle Burning"
"Some Old Lover's Ghost"
"The Sound of My Own Voice"

Small Wonders

DAYLE A. DERMATIS

SOUL'S
ROAD
PRESS

Small Wonders:
A Delightful Collection of
Ten Short-Short Speculative Fiction Stories

Dayle A. Dermatis

Print edition published 2015 by Soul's Road Press.

First Edition

ISBN-13: 978-0692364994 (trade paperback)
ISBN-10: 0692364994 (trade paperback)

Inquiries should be addressed to
Soul's Road Press
info@soulsroadpress.com
http://www.soulsroadpress.com

Cover image © frenta / Bigstockphoto
Logo designed by Designs by Trapdoor

Table of Contents

Small
Wonders

DAYLE A. DERMATIS

INTRODUCTION

This is a collection of short-short stories, so I've resolved not to let my introduction go longer than a page. Wish me luck.

It wasn't until I pulled the stories together and looked at the list that I realized how these stories span my writing career. The oldest story here, "What Dragons Prefer," was published in 1994 (and, incidentally, was my first professionally published story), and the most recent, "The Pumpkin-Carving Contest" was published in 2014.

I'm writing this introduction on the first day of 2015. I'm excited to see what my next twenty years of writing brings.

I hope you'll be with me for the journey!

—*Dayle A. Dermatis*
January 1, 2015

THE POWER TO CHANGE
THE SHAPE OF THE LAND

A geas bound her; she was bound never to harm the King with her sorceries.

Not even when he held a knife to her throat.

The brute force was enough to subdue her. He had left his men at the base of the tower, away from the night's storm, and entered her study alone, slamming the door back and placing the blade against her skin before she could react.

His entry had surprised her; his methods had not. This new King had risen to power by slaying everyone in his way. Even innocent children died and simple farms burned under his quest for the throne.

"You are a sorceress—a revered magician." He demanded agreement rather than asking the question.

"I am, your Grace."

His leather armor, soaked from the rain, stank of cow and days of sweat and the blood of helpless women. "There is something I seek, something you can help me gain. If you cannot…"

His sour breath brushed her cheek like a malevolent spirit on the longest night of year.

"What is it you seek, your Grace?" Her voice sounded distant. She had to remain composed.

"It is my desire to rule completely," he said. "I want the power to do that."

As he spoke, his hand tightened on the knife. The blade, warm from being carried close to him, scraped against her skin.

"And you believe that I have this power?"

"I know that sorcery is vast. As your King, I command that you use your sorcerous talents to help me."

She considered what she knew of him. He had used sorceresses in his campaign—in fact, she had known several of the women who had died, their deaths a small percentage of the total slaughter—so he wasn't ignorant of their existence. But he was ignorant of the extent of their abilities, and he was suspicious of sorcery.

"Then you also know that I cannot—I am unable—to harm you with those sorceries." She spoke with complete honesty; the geas that had been set upon her kind long ago to keep them from rising against the ruler of the land held her, no matter how she felt about him. "Your Grace, I am but a simple woman, and I live alone as my studies require: surely I pose so little of a threat to you that you can feel safe without your blade at my throat."

The quill had fallen when he had grabbed her. Her ink-stained fingers, laying carefully complacent on the desk, seemed as distant as her voice.

He complied. Still, no geas bound him as it did her. Slowly, so as not to startle him, she turned in her seat.

Outside, distant, beneath the hiss of the rain, she heard the low boom of the surf.

"Tell me of the power that you seek." The more time she had...she wasn't quite sure how that would help her. She had no illusion that anyone would rescue her. She lived far enough outside the town that no one would be venturing here on this wretched, storm-soaked night. She had purposely chosen this location because it was remote, for her year of reflection, a time of study and meditation every sorceress had after her seventh year of magic.

"I want the power to change this land—to change the shape of this land," he said, and his voice grew rough with the passion of his dream. "I want a power that men fear, and cannot overcome."

She closed her eyes. If she granted his wish, the land as it was now known would be forever, brutally, destroyed:

trampled and bludgeoned and burned by a man who cared for nothing but power.

If she denied him, she would die…but her death was hardly a hindrance to his goal. He would simply continue on until he found someone who would help him.

A choice—and soon, else he would take the choice from her, kill her, and be on his way.

"I will take you to something of great power," she said finally.

"And I will gain power from it?" he asked, guardedly eager.

"It cannot give you power, but it can teach you about power."

"You swear, sorceress, that I will learn power from this thing?"

She shook her head, carefully, feeling the memory of the blade hot against her throat.

"I can make no guarantees about your own ability to learn," she said. "I can swear that this thing has very great power—the power to change the land, a power that men fear greatly. I can swear that much can be learned from it. If you are a perceptive man, then you will learn about power from it."

He considered her words, the only sound that of sapfire spitting in the grate. She waited, still, her chest barely stirred by her breaths. He would either choose to trust her, or he would kill her.

"Very well, sorceress," he said finally. "Take me to this power."

A breath of relief, and then, "There are two final conditions," she said quietly. Vaguely, she was astonished at how steady and calm she sounded—but she knew if she gave any hint of uncalm, he would slit her throat and leave her body to seep lifeblood into the worn floorboards.

His fingers twitched on the knife. "You said nothing of conditions."

"There are two," she repeated. "They must be met, or this thing cannot be done. You have no chance of learning otherwise."

"What are they?" he snapped.

"You and I must go alone, and you may bring no weapons." The latter wasn't much to save her, she knew—he could snap her neck between his burly hands as easily and thoughtlessly as breaking a branch for kindling. But perhaps, in a small way, it would give her more authority.

He growled low, in the back of his throat, and despite herself, she flinched.

But, as she'd gambled, his lust for power outweighed his common sense.

"Take me," he commanded.

*

The rain had ceased, leaving the early morning sodden as if the clouds were made of unwrung towels. As requested, he arrived at the docks alone and unarmed.

"Must we travel in that thing?" He eyed her small boat suspiciously. He was a land-born man, unused to sea travel, unlearned of the sea. That, she knew, was the only thing that enabled her to do this—the fact that she had grown up by the sea, and he had not.

"I know of no other way to take you to your goal," she said mildly, less afraid now. His power-lust had already betrayed him; he wouldn't turn back now.

They sailed until no shore was in sight, and then she brought the boat around and fixed the sails so they bobbed, gently, on the waves.

"What now, sorceress?" he snapped.

She held a hand out toward the sea. "Now you must get in the water."

To his credit, he showed no sign of fear. In that way, he was a strong leader of men. But he also ruled by fear.

He leaned toward her, and she met his gaze with as much unfear as she could.

"I cannot swim," he said. Which she had supposed, and hoped.

"This is the only way," she responded. "Here, I will tie this rope about your waist, so—" and she securely looped it around him "—and the other end of it to the boat." She deftly flipped the rope into a knot, and tugged at the knot to show him its sturdiness.

Again, her instinct of him proved true: his lust for power outweighed his common sense, and he slipped into the chill winter swells.

"Where is this thing that will show me power?" he called out to her, gripping the rope, splash-paddling in something of a circle to search in all directions.

She took a deep breath. The sea salt seared her nostrils. He didn't understand. She supposed that somewhere, somehow, she'd hoped that he would, that somewhere, humanity would prevail. But he didn't, and it didn't, so she had to continue.

With a wrist-flick she released the knot that held the rope to the boat. She'd based so much of this on the hope that he wouldn't know knots.

"The ocean is a powerful force, feared by all," she shouted as she snapped a sail up before he could grab the edge of the boat. The skiff began skimming the water for home.

His men-at-arms would be waiting when she docked. She was calm in that knowledge. What mattered was that he couldn't hurt anyone now: his evil ways would not continue.

She wondered if they would give her time to explain before they killed her.

The ocean was a powerful force; its waves ate at the shore and changed the shape of the land. Wise men learned its power and respected and feared it.

And truly wise men understood that there were forces far greater than them, power far greater than they could ever possess.

THE PUMPKIN-CARVING CONTEST

My name is Annemarie Ling-Hernandez, and I am in Mrs. Stefan's class. I live in Mount Pleasant, New York. This is my essay about my entry in the pumpkin-carving contest.

I would really, really, really like to win this contest because I never win anything ever. Like at Halloween in school when we play musical pumpkins. It's like musical chairs except that there aren't any chairs, just construction-paper pumpkins on the floor, and when the music stops we each have to grab a pumpkin. Every year for as long as I can remember Jacob Leister and me are the last two people and there's one pumpkin on the floor and we both grab for it and it rips, and he always has the bigger half, so he gets the prize.

And it's usually the one I made. I know because I always put the biggest green stem on.

How I carved my pumpkin:

First we went to the pumpkin patch on Route 9 and I looked and looked to find the perfect pumpkin ever. A couple of times my dad looked at his phone and asked if I had found it yet, and then my mom hit him in the arm and told him this was a special thing and someday I wouldn't want to do this anymore. Of course I will! My mom took a picture of me in the pumpkin patch and then she went back to reading stuff on her phone.

So anyway, I found the perfect pumpkin, it was round and not lopsided and had a really long stem.

My mom made me put it on the back porch on top of lots of newspaper, and my dad scooped out all the squishy insides which made me glad because I didn't want to touch them.

Then I sat there looking at the pictures that came with the pumpkin carving kit trying to decide what I wanted to do. I'd mostly decided to do a cat when the man showed up.

I'm supposed to come in when it gets dark, but the porch light was on and I figured it was okay if someone was with me.

Anyway, he said I should look at it from all angles, and I didn't understand what he meant, but then he said I should roll it onto its side, and when I did I could see that the stem looked like a long nose.

I know we're not supposed to get any help with our pumpkins except if we can't use the knife, but he didn't do any of the carving, he just made suggestions, and that's okay, right? I could see that it looked like a nose, and all he did was say make the mouth bigger or made the eyes egg-shaped with points at the edges, not round.

When I was done he said he wanted to take it with him. I cried because it was my only pumpkin and my parents were too busy to take me back to the pumpkin patch. And he said it was okay as long as I gave it back to him after I turned it in for this contest. So I need to have my jack-o-lantern back so I can give it to the nice man.

I really, really hope I win!

Annemarie Ling-Hernandez

*

Addendum from Heather Stefan to the Judging Committee:

I know this looks incredibly sophisticated for one of the children in my class. I did call the parents in for a conference, and they both swore they didn't help Annemarie with the project at all. Given how wrapped up they are in their jobs, I'm inclined to believe them. They acted like they'd never seen it before, even though Mr. Hernandez carried the jack-o-lantern in for Annemarie.

They are not familiar with any man who might have helped her and, indeed, are disturbed (as am I) that a stranger approached her that night—especially given that their back yard is fenced in.

I have asked Annemarie about the man, and she has been unable to describe him with any degree of certainty. She says that it was dark and she couldn't see his face. When pressed, she said that it looked like he didn't have a head—clearly, she didn't want to continue the conversation, so I let it drop.

Although Annemarie isn't prone to fanciful tales, I can only assume she was inspired by the artwork we have of Ichabod Crane in the school library: the long, crooked nose; the wide mouth; the way his eyebrows are uneven, all echo the facial features of Crane, almost eerily so.

Of course, we don't tell the stories about the Headless Horseman in class, as it may be too disturbing for children this age. However, it's always possible Annemarie heard the tale elsewhere. I asked her, but she seemed unaware of the legend.

Yes, the work she did on the pumpkin is beyond what we expect from this age. Although she hasn't shown latent artistic talent before, it's possible that Annemarie is finally coming into her own, especially given the creative essay she provided. I recommend that she be allowed to join the advanced art class if a spot comes free.

*

I gave the man the pumpkin today. He put it on his head, and nodded, and I laughed because the pumpkin nodding looked funny, and he said thank you and that he would see me next year. Then he got on his big black horse and rode away, and I ran inside and told my mom and dad, and they told me not to make up stories that weren't true.

I don't care. I won the pumpkin carving contest!!! I've never won anything before!!! I put the blue ribbon over my bed so I can see it all the time. It's even better than the candy I'm going to get when I go trick-or-treating tonight.

CYCLES

My moon cycles started today.

My mother had asked me to tell her when I became a woman, but she was gone before I woke. That wasn't new; her duties required her to be up and out by dawn.

It was Wednesday, the day I always took a satchel of food to my grandmother, who lived on the far side of the valley. Nothing unusual there.

No, something else was different, something I knew I didn't understand, but felt, deep in my bones, that I would understand very soon.

Perhaps too soon.

I was a woman now. When I told my mother tonight, she would arrange to take me to town, to the circle of woman, for a celebration

Today, though, the world seemed clearer, as I teetered on the cusp of knowledge. I stuck out my tongue, tasting the air for a hint. I savored spring and a hint of something indefinable.

I shrugged on my scarlet wool coat and hoisted the heavy satchel—fresh-baked bread brimming with oats and seeds, crumbly white cheese, a newly killed chicken, some asparagus—onto my back. By the door was a walking stick that my mother had taught me to use as a cudgel as well, just in case.

The woods are not always a safe haven, even for those who've always lived here.

Spring on the breeze, and the buttercups and bluebells that fluttered at the side of the path were brighter than I ever remembered seeing them.

Off the path, ivy twined around the tree trunks, obscuring the bark. It carpeted the ground as well, creating a haven for small creatures. The dark, glossy leaves skittered with their movements.

Everything was darker there, the sun struggling harder and failing more often than not to pierce the thick canopy of branches.

But I had no fear of the woods, and why would I? For all the warnings I'd been given, I'd grown up here, playing at my mother's feet while she worked.

My heightened senses slowed my feet as I delighted over things I'd seen and heard and smelled all my life. And so, that day, I was too late to save my grandmother.

There was blood, so much blood, hot and crimson and coppery-stanched like the blood that flowed out of me, making me a woman.

The wolf's head whipped around, and he pinned me with his black-eyed, glittering gaze. A knitting needle buried in his side showed me my grandmother had tried to protect herself, to no avail. His upper lip curled, revealing sharp yellowed teeth, and he snarled. The cudgel fell from my numb fingers to clatter on the hardwood floor.

He turned, and through the blood I smelled damp, dirty fur. He crouched, muscles bunching to leap. To attack. To kill me, because I'd learned nothing and dropped the only weapon I had.

The front door banged open again, and I heard a shout, followed by ululation as my mother ran into the room.

The wolf, in mid-bound, didn't stand a chance. My mother buried her axe in his neck, half-severing his head. The new spray of hot blood sent me to my knees, retching.

When I finished, my mother knelt beside me, handing me a cup of cool water. It tasted better than I could have imagined, full of life like the spring air and the bluebells and the ivy.

And with that knowledge came more. I hauled myself up and faced her.

"You knew the wolf would come today."

"I didn't. I suspected it, though. It's not the first time we've met. Once before for me, twice before for your grandmother." She didn't look over at her mother's body, but I sensed that she already knew what she would see.

"I…I don't understand." I did, and yet didn't, secrets on the tip of my tongue, on the edge of the breeze, just out of reach.

"We each must face the wolf three times: As maiden," and she rested a hand on my shoulder, broad and comforting, "mother, and crone."

"But he's dead," I said stupidly.

"He will be reborn."

I swallowed. "So, when you're the grandmother, you'll…die?"

I was patient through her silence. "Not necessarily," she said finally. "It has been that way thus far, but there is always a chance. I didn't get here soon enough. My duties took me deeper into the woods than usual, and when I realized it was to be today." Through her touch I felt her anguish, her deep loss. "But perhaps I will be stronger when my time comes, and I can stop him before he kills me. Or you can. Or…"

"Or my daughter can." I pondered that. "How long has this been going on?"

"Since the dawn of time, or so I've been told," she said. "The cycle has always been."

"There must be a way to break the cycle," I said.

My mother didn't smile, but she cupped my cheek. "I believe if anyone can find a way, it will be you," she said, before turning to haul the wolf's carcass towards the door.

I picked up the cudgel from the floor. I would practice with it, and with my grandmother's sword, and with my mother's axe. I would become the woodskeeper after my own daughter would be born (years from now, yet I knew I mustn't delay my training). My mother would move to my grandmother's cottage.

And, I vowed, we would fight the wolf together, all three of us. Separate, we failed again and again. As one, we would prevail.

CREATIVE ARSENAL

My steptfather is a beast.

No, no, he doesn't beat my mother; he doesn't try anything funny with me. He's a *beast*.

Believe me, I've been reading science fiction and horror since I was eight. I know these things.

Mom, of course, doesn't have a clue. I don't know why she married him, except that she was lonely after Dad died. I can understand that. When you're a sophomore and your body hasn't "budded" yet and you're the only reason the town library buys any new science fiction, you understand "lonely."

However, even Mom was becoming a bit concerned about my stepdad's frequent nights "away on business trips." I'd seen that worried look in her eyes when he announced that he's going. She just hasn't clued in to the fact that these "business trips" always coincide with the full moon. Or that he never takes a change of clothes, just a briefcase that I'd opened once when he wasn't around. It was empty.

It took me about four months to put all the clues together and see the furry puzzle for what it was. For example, the random unexplained cow deaths and disappearances around the county. There were mutters about how the despised Eisenglass Mountains Preservation Agency ("those tree-hugging whoopies" was the usual phrase) had probably re-introduced wolves or mountain lions into the forests without telling the residents. But wolves and big cats didn't ravage a cow's throat and leave the prime meat behind.

Then there was the fact that all of the farm dogs stopped treating Rowdy the German shepherd as the alpha male and starting acting that way towards Paul. The negative reaction of Buster and Crabbe, the barn cats, to Paul was even more dramatic. Even the cows seemed nervous.

Beastly, eh? (Sorry. I'm trying to develop more of a sense of humor in the hopes of gaining more popularity. As if any guy at school will notice me until I "bud.") So anyway, you see the problem. Since Mom is blind to it, it's up to me.

One morning, as I was in the bathroom getting ready for school, I caught a sight in the mirror of the white flash of my teeth, newly released from their prison of braces. They reminded me of Stepbeast. I frowned. My options, according to my research, were slim. I despised the thought of a gun—I had visions of being carted off to juvenile hall—and besides, where was I going to get the special ammunition? I wondered if some other type of projectile-shooter would work. What did people do about this before guns?

Walking to school, alternately pondering the problem and my first period math test, I kicked at some litter someone had tossed on the shoulder. It bounced down the road ahead of me, banging with drunken atonality, before careening into the ditch. I looked—and looked again—and then I whooped with laughter.

It was a long shot, but it just might work.

*

I bribed a senior to get me what I needed, and then I waited for a Tuesday night, Mom's school board night. (Yes, on top of being a geek, I have a mother on the school board.) I made sure it coincided with a quarter moon, too, thank you very much. When Stepbeast started making motions of getting up for a beer, I leapt out of my chair and offered to get it for him.

He stared at me. I've never been mean to him, but I've never been outright nice to him, either.

I shrugged in what I hoped was a nonchalant way. "No problem, Paul." (I refuse to call him "Dad." Please, allow me to retain some dignity.) "I was on my way to get a soda."

The beast wasn't stupid; I could tell he was a little suspicious. In the kitchen, I took a deep breath, then popped open the beer and poured it into a mug. I stared at the foamy head. This was really pushing it, but I was fresh out of other ideas.

As he raised the mug to his face I poised to flee, not wanting to watch if it worked—or even if it didn't. Just before he took a sip, though, he paused, and sniffed dubiously.

My stomach plummeted to somewhere in the vicinity of my shins. He always drank Budweiser, darn it. Always. Of course he'd notice the difference.

"Mom bought a six-pack of Miller by mistake," I improvised. I hated to blame her, but with any luck, he wouldn't be around to grump at her when she got home.

He made a face, but took a swallow anyway.

I bolted for the kitchen.

An animal howl spiraled the house, filled with agony and despair. I leaned against the fridge and sank down, wrapping my arms around my knees. The cold of the linoleum seeped through my jeans. The tormented howl faded away, but echoed in my head, in my bones.

Finally I dared to creep back to the living room. Stepbeast was slumped in the easy chair, the mug fallen from his dangling fingers. It was going to be a bitch to get the smell of beer out of the carpet. Sorry, Mom.

I poked tentatively at his bicep. When he didn't move, I checked for a pulse. He was dead. The way his head was tilted, I could see hair sprouting from his ears. Yech. Mom's taste had better improve.

I went back into the kitchen and looked at the empty can. Coors Light, the Silver Bullet. What was the slogan? "It's the right beer now"?

I tucked the rest of the beer way in the back of the pantry, where Mom usually forgets to clean. Then I went upstairs to study for tomorrow's chemistry exam, wondering how Bad Company's *Holy Water* album would work against vampires.

THE SULTAN'S SONS

Two women gave birth in the palace that night. Hot sands shifted in the desert outside, but a cool breeze sifted through the silk hangings of each room to trace the ripples on their bellies and taste the sweat on their brows.

Two healthy boys were born that night. But one was the son of the sultan's wife, and the other the son of the sultan's concubine. Both would be raised in wealth and comfort, but only one would rule.

*

The first oil lamps had been lit, and were already perfuming the air as the servant slipped from the room. No breeze wafted through the hangings, colored ruby and emerald and sapphire, in the grasping heat just before sundown. Moisture beaded like sweat on the heavy glasses containing cool fruit drinks.

The sultan sat forward on his amber-crusted throne, and gazed at his two sons.

"I have known for some time," he said, "that there has been a conspiracy to kill me." He gestured behind him, where just outside the window a row of heads on spikes wore crimson halos from the setting sun. "Men have died in my quest to learn who is responsible."

"Innocent men," commented the son of his concubine.

The sultan glanced at him sharply. "Apparently so, for none confessed," he said. He toyed with a tassel on the cushion beneath him, a casual motion that both sons knew was, in truth, calculating. "You have often spoken out against my practices, which you call cruel, son. This brings me to wonder if perhaps you are the one responsible."

"Oh, father," said the son of the sultan's wife, stretching languidly on the cushions at the sultan's left hand. "The truth may as well be known in the little time left. Know your conspirator, father: It is I who has sought to take your life."

The sultan's only reaction was a tightening of his fingers on the tassel.

"So," he said, "you confess. But why is it not folly to confess when you have failed?"

"But I haven't failed, father." The son of the sultan's wife lifted the etched sapphire-like goblet from the tray where the sultan had placed it. "The poison in your drink took me a year to find, all the money I had saved and more to buy it, and no doubt my immortal soul to the sorcerer who concocted the foul stuff. You should feel its effects beginning already: your breath more difficult, perhaps, your heart beating slower. Even if you called for your guards right now, they would see only a death natural for a man of your years. The poison cannot be traced or detected."

"Why?" The son of the sultan's concubine leapt from the cushions at the sultan's right hand, the long curved sword flashing in the light of the lamps.

"Because I wish to rule unfettered," the son of the sultan's wife said simply. "I have learned well from our father's ways, while you have questioned the firm hand with which he rules."

He watched impassively as the sword swung closer—and continued to watch, impassive, as the son of the sultan's concubine fell with a soundless cry to the floor.

"I suspected that your love for our father would lead you to try and kill me," said the son of the sultan's wife, removing the sword from the other man's hand and placing the tip of it on his chest. A flick of his wrist, and the cloth parted with no more sound than that which came from the fallen man's mouth.

"The poison I chose for you was different," explained the son of the sultan's wife, now placing the tip of the sword on his brother's abdomen. "You are simply paralyzed, and would live except that soon, you will wish you could beg for death. I must have an example to show others what will happen if they dare defy me."

With the same noise as before, the sword began to part flesh.

*

The sultan was renowned for many things, most of them whispered in fear and abhorrence. One exception to this was the palace garden, because of its unique architectural feature of being on the roof. Because it was on a lower roof, it was bordered on three sides by higher walls, and thus the fig and date trees received enough shade to bloom and prosper.

The garden had originally been a single, open area, but now a low wall, perhaps the height of a woman's knees, bisected it. A low wall, seemingly inconsequential. But it was a necessary barrier.

The wife of the sultan and the concubine of the sultan spent little time near the wall.

Tonight was another exception. The sultan's wife's dark silk robes and veils made little impression in the night, whether by sight or sound. She seemed unaware of the presence of the sultan's concubine, who stood on the other side of the wall, gazing at the silver moon on the horizon, shaped so much like a sharp, curved sword blade. The sultan's wife also seemed unaware of the sultan's concubine.

Both knew.

The weeping of the sultan's wife made no more impression on the silence than had the silken breath of her robes. But finally the sultan's concubine broke out, soft but harsh, "Why do you weep? It is not you who has lost a son this night."

It was the first time one had ever spoken to the other.

"Would that the gods of fire had seen fit to kill my son," replied the sultan's wife. "He is as good as dead—he is as evil and cruel as his father—something I have feared since his birth. I wish more than anything that he had died this night."

They were silent again, and for a time it seemed as though the conversation would not only be their first, but also their last.

Then the sultan's concubine spoke, the veil across her face shivering at her breath.

"I must confess to you now," she said. "You may have me killed when you hear my words, but even so, if they give you small comfort, perhaps you might choose to spare me."

A gust of wind sent clouds across the sky, catching on the sharp point of the moon like thin cloth about to tear beneath a sword's onslaught.

"It is not my son who died this night, but yours," said the sultan's concubine, emotion not present in her voice, for that was a gift to those of greater station than she. "I had no wish to have my son grow up in the shadow of another just as I have spent my life in the shadow of you—both loved equally, but yet never equal.

"I wanted him to rule.

"So, on the night of our sons' birth, I rose from my birthing pillows and crept into the nursery, and switched the babes in their beds. Truly, your son was raised as mine, as the son of a concubine, and was killed this night."

The sultan's wife began to laugh. At first it was a sharp bark, but as it persisted, it grew more shrill and frantic, until the sultan's concubine began to believe that they sultan's wife had truly gone mad in her grief. Finally she subsided into harsh sobs, and then, eventually, when she could speak:

"I, too, have a confession," she said. "When I spoke, I was not mourning the life of an evil son, but the death of a good one. I spoke to hide my own deception. On the selfsame night that you switched your child with mine so that yours could rule, so did I creep into the nursery to replace one babe with another so that my son would not rule. I feared my son becoming evil like his father, and I thought that if he were raised as the son of a concubine, he would learn more gentle ways.

"So you see, we both wished different lives for our sons, and in doing so, we gave them the very lives we feared they would lead."

A dry wind blew up the side of the building, bringing with it the gritty sense of fear from the city outside.

"Who would have thought," whispered the sultan's concubine, "that we would have been of such like mind as to make the same choice?"

The sultan's wife failed to answer. After another endless moment with the stars glittering like the sultan's favorite jeweled cups, each moved silently, finally, away from the wall.

A MATTER OF PERSPECTIVE

When George arrived, I was doing what every self-respecting student does after the day's classes are over: I was holed up in the college pub, facing the watery remains of the third draught of that typical poor beer that every college pub serves because the students are trapped here and will buy the available alcohol no matter what it tastes like.

So help me, George fit the stereotype of his major so well: The disheveled, poorly shorn hair; the pale skin from spending too much time inside; the ink stain in the pocket of his shirt. But despite all that, despite his studies about which he talks too much and about which I understand nothing, I like him. And that's why, as his squinting eyes searched the dim room with a hint of minor desperation, I waved at him.

"Barrett!" he said when he reached my booth in the corner. "I thought I might find you here."

"I'm becoming too predictable," I commented lazily, but he missed the comment, probably because it didn't rise above the typically distorted music. He slid into the booth across from me. He set his hands on either side of him to lean forward; then his face grimaced in a decidedly sour look, and he wiped the stale beer off one hand onto his trouser leg.

"I heard the most amusing joke today," George said, "and I just had to share it with you."

"Do tell," I said. After failing today's physics test, I needed some levity. I even had hope that, despite coming from George's odd sense of humor, I'd find the joke funny.

"Okay." He set his hands firmly on the table, fingers twined. "A student was walking along the road when he came across a talking frog. The frog said, 'I've been enchanted. Kiss me and I'll return to my natural form of a beautiful princess!'"

Over George's shoulder, I caught the eye of a buxom blonde I recognized from my ancient history class. I gave her my most winning smile, to which, oddly, she seemed immune. With a resigned glance at her retreating bottom, I turned my attention back to the story.

"Well, the student picked up the frog, but he didn't kiss it. So the frog said, 'Kiss me and allow me to return to my natural form, and I will spend the week with you.'"

"I'm really not seeing where this is going," I began, but George bounced in his seat, and rather than have him attract attention by that, I set my lips together and nodded for him to continue. He pushed up his slipping spectacles.

"Well, the student didn't do anything, so *then* the frog said, 'When I return to my natural form, I'll also give you anything your heart desires.' But the student still didn't do anything."

This was bordering on the ridiculous, and not in the way he intended. I was about to say so, but George was obviously getting close to the punch line, by the way he was nearly quivering with excitement.

"The enchanted frog cried, 'What's wrong with you? All you have to do is kiss me once, and I'll turn into a beautiful princess who'll stay with you for a week and grant you everything your heart desires!'

"And the student said, 'I'm a computer major. I don't have time for a girlfriend, but a talking frog is really neat.'"

George stopped and looked at me expectantly. It took me a moment to realize he'd finished the joke.

"I don't get it," I said flatly.

"But Barrett, don't you see? He's a computer major!"

I shook my head. "I'm sorry—what's a computer?"

"Barrett, I know I've told you about the people who—"

I was losing patience, but I cut him off as gently as I could. "And what is so interesting about a talking frog? They're a dime a dozen."

George threw up his hands in dismay, a comical gesture that would have made me laugh had I consumed a few more beers. I rose, clapped him on his bony shoulder, and fought my way through the crowd to the front door, where I obtained my horse from the stable across the street (paying an exorbitant parking fee, but what's a poor student to do?) and headed home.

So help me, no matter how long I stay at the university, I'll never understand people who major in Magic, especially those with an emphasis in Interdimensional Studies.

ACCIDENTAL VICTIM

I heard the terrible, shrieking sound of rending metal a moment before I came upon the accident.

My windows were down; the early evening air was silent and still, warm. My first instinct was to turn my car around and flee, and then I was ashamed. I rounded the corner and saw the other white car, its front buried around a tree, its rear half-filling the lane. I pulled in behind it.

My door resisted opening. *Needs to be oiled*, I thought; then, *what a horrible thing to think about right now.* I approached the wreck, slowly.

I heard no noise from the car; it was as if the horrible sound of the accident had frightened all others into silence. Even the summer crickets kept silent. The trees growing close to the edges of the one-lane dirt road made the insides of the car shadowy and dim.

I looked in the driver's window. The woman was dead. She looked familiar to me somehow, but the memory skittered around in my brain, too fast to catch and see. Her wide, sightless eyes stared at nothing, and a line of blood trickled from the glass-spattered gash on her forehead. I swallowed hard, pulled back.

A sudden movement in the backseat startled me, and I jerked, stomach wincing. I peered in. Two children stared back: a girl of about six, a boy of about two. They were belted in, and looked unharmed.

"Hello," I said softly. "Are you okay?"

A pair of silky blonde heads solemnly nodded, eyes never leaving me.

"Then let's get you two out of the car."

The door had buckled in from the crash; I had to brace my foot against the side of the car to wrench to it open. The boy was closer to me, and I fumbled with his seatbelt. He crawled out, the girl following. She hesitated at the door.

"What about her?" she asked, pointing at the driver's seat.

How could I tell the children? They weren't even old enough to understand what death meant. I forced a smile on my face as I turned to them, blocking their view of the front seat.

"I think the best thing is for us to go get help— to tell someone what happened, okay?" Trusting nods.

I looked at my car, dusty and dirty even from the short drive. There wasn't enough room to turn it around in the narrow lane, and it wouldn't fit past the other car. There was a gas station about half a mile back, at the intersection where this lane started, so I took one child's hands in each of mine.

"What's your name?" I asked the girl.

"Melissa." She had the slightest of lisps.

"And yours?"

"Gorb."

"Gorb?"

"His name is Gordon," Melissa said with all the authority of an older sister. "He can't say 'Gordon' yet."

"Okay, Melissa and Gorb, let's go for a walk."

They faltered about halfway there, of course, unused to walking so far. I remembered a roll of Lifesavers I'd bought earlier, and dug them from my pocket. Gorb gently insisted on a red one. I carried him a short ways, and he gave me a brilliant, cherry-stained smile. He squirmed down as we neared our destination.

We emerged from the trees. A street light flashed on, spangled off a gas pump. I saw with relief that a police car was parked just outside the mini-mart.

We were halfway across the parking lot when the mini-mart's door flew open and a woman emerged with the police officer.

"That's her!" the woman cried, pointing at me. "That's the woman who stole my babies!"

Mommy!" Melissa said.

Mommy? Then who had been driving the car?

Melissa and Gorb tugged at my hands like minnows on a line, and I released them. The woman ran forward and dropped to her knees as they reached her, grabbing one in each arm and squeezing tightly.

The policeman approached me, hand not quite on his gun, dark eyes wary.

"Officer, I don't know what she's talking about," I said, confused. "I came upon an accident about half a mile that way—" I nodded my head to indicate the direction "—and the children were in the backseat."

"Brought us back," Gorb said clearly, pointing at me.

"She's the one, officer!" the woman insisted. I shrugged helplessly.

He sighed, glancing at each of us.

"I think we need to go for a ride," he said.

I got into the front seat with him, because the woman commandeered the backseat for herself and the children, hugging them to herself when I walked by. I glanced back and frowned; she cuddled Gorb on her lap instead of safely belting him in.

My frown deepened when, moments later, the squad car pulled in behind the accident. There was only one car, the one that had crashed. I got out and stared at it.

My car?

I forced my suddenly weakened legs to take me to the driver's side window. My own face stared back, dead and unseeing, the trickle of blood now clotted and black.

*

I turned, but it was as though a film of dark gauze separated me from the others.

"Mommy?" Melissa asked, tugging at her hand. "Where did the nice lady go?"

The darkness swirled into colors, achingly vibrant. Too beautiful.

"No," I said, when I understood. "No, I don't deserve this."

"But you do," said a voice—many voices?—sounding warm and forgiving. "You brought the children back."

"But I didn't know—I didn't remember…taking them." I remembered now. The horror of it made me want to retch.

"Would it have made any difference if you had remembered?"

I thought. "No," I said, and I knew they sensed the honesty in my reply.

"Well, then, come along." Gentle humor in the kind voices. "Let's go for a walk."

RETURN

From the moon, earth was a blue marble. Or so they said. Clutching her handheld computer, Kayley turned away from the window and drifted to the sofa, where the fibers in her clothes reacted with the furniture's fibers, preventing her from floating away at the slightest movement. Marbles didn't work well in this gravity.

Upon her parents' death last week, a file had automatically downloaded to her computer. She hadn't been able to read it yet. Every time she thought about it, she smelled her mother's sage incense and heard her father's drumming, and she cried. Which was ironic, because growing up, she'd been embarrassed by her parents' pagan beliefs and practices. Couldn't they let it go? The earth was destroyed by pollution and careless, uncaring people; prayers to Gaia were useless now.

In death, they'd had to let it go. It was gone, and so were they. Kayley took a deep breath and keyed the file open.

"The earth, the air, the fire, the water; return, return, return, return…"

Tears filled her eyes at the song, her parents' voices.

She managed not to bawl until the message finished. They loved her, they were sorry for embarrassing her, and they charged her with keeping something sacred.

*

She didn't expect what she found inside the storage facility. Her parents' artwork, perhaps, or an altar. No, the storage unit had been made into a greenhouse, and contained four seedlings, labeled Rowan, Oak, Ash, and Thorn. Her inheritance was four trees.

*

When the trees started talking to her, Kayley thought she'd gone mad.

The earth, the air, the fire, the water; return, return, return, return…

She tried to talk to a co-worker, but Loren laughed, and then the psychdocs were asking for an appointment. She avoided them. How could she explain to them that the trees wanted to go home?

"The Goddess—Gaia, earth—is the Mother of all life," her parents had said. They had rescued the seedlings, hidden them in stasis until they were ready to start growing—until they were ready to be taken back to earth, to their Mother, to grow and flourish and heal the wounds.

Kayley didn't remember the earth; knew only life on the moon. It hadn't been very friendly to her. Her parents' beliefs had caused the others to shun them, the children to taunt her. But their house—embarrassing as it might have been—had been a haven of lushness and color in the bare, stark base. Even from a distance, the blue of earth enticed her now. The soil in the trees' containers must smell so much more pungent there.

*

In the stolen ship, watching the blue earth grow larger, Kayley and the trees sang.

The earth, the air, the fire, the water; return, return, return, return...

THE DEVIL WENT DOWN
TO THE SUNSET STRIP

It was the conversation that every mother dreads having with her teenage daughter. The 80s were back in style, and I'd let her paw through an old box of my things for her Halloween costume. (Ouch.)

Then she came out of my bedroom holding a worn, torn black sweatshirt and a cassette tape and asked, "Mom, who's Angrrr Management?"

Crap. How was I supposed to answer that?

Could I be honest with her? Well, sweetie, they were an up-and-coming hair metal band and I was their groupie.

Or the full truth: Also, I saved the idiots from selling their souls to the Devil.

*

I slid into the curved, red-leather-covered booth next to Stixxx. (He was so proud of that nickname.

They all had ones with triple letters to go with the band name, but he was also the drummer. Plus, triple-X, get it?) Although it was only late afternoon, I was pretty sure that was Tommy Lee in the back corner pounding back shots. Hard to say, really, because he was half-covered by two groupies of his own.

"Shit," Keith Singerrr (the vocalist—big surprise) muttered. "Ono's here."

"Knock it off," Jefff said, punching him in the arm. Keith flipped him the bird, but shut up.

Keith was mad because I'd thrown him over for Jefff, who played bass. Let's face it (not that I'd tell my daughter this), I'd slept with them all at least once, once or twice with more than one at a time. But Jefff was my favorite, and let's face it, you want to deal with big egos? Musicians' egos are bigger than their hair, and Angrrr Management was well on their way to single-handedly destroying the ozone layer.

I wish I'd thought of buying stock in Aqua Net.

Keith didn't have a leg to stand on, anyway. He was crashing at my place like the rest of them, passing out on the living room floor, the sofa, the other half of my narrow bed ever night. I fed them ramen and hot dogs, kept them supplied with Jack and guitar strings, cleaned up their puke, made sure they got to gigs on time.

Hell, I even bought their makeup.

"I thought you were at work," Jefff said, fondling my knee under the table. At least, I thought it was his hand.

"Yeah, small problem there. You know how I was handing out your demo tape? Against Tower Records' policies. They fired my ass."

Oh, yeah, I'd paid for their demo session, too.

I'd gone to the apartment, and Gina, who either lived next door or was the building's favorite hooker-on-call, told me the band said they were going to the Rainbow Room.

"No problem," Jefff said, his glossed smile wide. "We're hittin' the big time. We just got a manager!"

Weird as it sounds, until that moment I hadn't noticed the suit in the booth. Then, my eyes still wanted to slide over him rather than focus on him.

My gut clenched. Something was very wrong.

"You signed already?"

"Mr. Nicholas had the gnarliest idea, too," Keith said. "We all got tattoos to celebrate."

Four forearms slapped down on the table to display four bright red tridents. Because the company, I swiftly learned, was called Pitchfork Promoters.

Angrrr Management were four talented guys. (They really were. I wasn't just some starry-eyed groupie; I knew decent music and I knew stage presence.) Talented, yes, and awfully pretty, all of them.

And every last one of them was dumber than a post.

Had they never *heard* of Robert Johnson?

Apparently not, because they'd gotten their tattoos at a parlor at the crossroads of Hollywood and Vine.

Van Halen's "Running With the Devil" was blaring through the club, and the band was whooping and toasting with shots and snorting lines (a celebratory present from Mr. Nicholas), and I closed my eyes and muttered, "Oh, hell."

I heard a low, otherworldly chuckle.

*

I went to Mr. Nicholas's office the next day, determined to do…something.

I wore the most suit-like professional outfit I had. Granted, it was pale pink and satiny, but the skirt came down below my knees (skinny, with a big slit up the back) and the blazer had some amazing shoulder pads that made me feel confident and strong.

Until I walked into his office, and he smiled a toothy smile and said with a body like mine, he could totally make me a star. Gag me with a spoon.

"I know who you are," I said. "Totally. So don't try to trick me." He probably would try, anyway. I hoped to hell I wouldn't mess up.

I asked if I could take a copy of the contract with me, but he said no. Damn. In the back of my trunk was a battered box of my first-year law books, including Contracts.

I'd gotten through a whole year before I ditched the school and started driving west.

So I did my best to ignore him while I poured through the tiny print legalese. There were pages and pages of it. I swallowed, fighting back panic.

"What does this mean?" I asked, pointing at a clause. "How can you guarantee to get them a major record deal?"

"Oh, that." He leaned back, the leather of his chair creaking, and clasped his hands behind his head. Obviously confident enough in his abilities that it wasn't worth lying to me. "Simple, really. Their Friday night gig at the Roxy? At my invitation, there'll be several record execs are in the audience. And I'll give the boys amazing talent, so the execs will have to bite."

In exchange, the contract's convoluted wording said, buried on page thirty-six, was each guy's soul.

"Is there anything I can do to convince you to break the deal?" I asked.

He sniffed. "You're hardly a virgin, but your soul's still sweet. Which one's your favorite? I'll let you trade your soul for his."

I'd've been offended if the lack-of-virginity part wasn't true. At any rate, as fond as I was of Jefff, I wasn't going to abandon the whole group. "Not good enough."

That oily smile again. "You could take me up on my offer to make you a star. You'd be even more fun than them."

"No!"

He leaned forward, scowling. I don't care what they say about hell being hot—the room dropped twenty degrees, I swear.

"Miss Patrick, you are trying my patience," he said. "This is supposed to be fun, and you're making it not fun anymore. So you know what I'm going to do? Friday night, after they get their record deal? That's when I'm taking their souls. They're all going to die."

*

Not if I could help it.

Fact was, I had enough drugs and alcohol in my system to believe I could take on the Devil. In the back of my mind, I knew that if I failed, he'd find some way to take my soul, but I was too—let's call it "focused"—to care.

I had only a day to pull it off.

Friday night, Angrrr Management played an incredible gig. There were some equipment flub-ups, sure, but they sounded totally bitchen'. Afterwards, in the closet that passed as a dressing room, they were approached by not one, not two, but three major labels.

I made them promise they wouldn't sign anything without me, and went out to the dance floor.

"I hope you've had your chance to say goodbye," Mr. Nicholas said, looking dapper in a pin-striped suit and skinny tie. "I'm afraid they're all going to be in a tragic, drug-fueled car accident tonight. No survivors."

"I don't think so," I shouted above the next band (something about roses and guns) who'd just taken the stage. "Your contract's invalid."

"Impossible," he hissed.

"Totally, dude. They didn't get the record contract because you helped them."

"I gave them exceptional musical talent."

"But nobody heard it. They were lip-synching. I turned off their amps and fed their demo recordings through." I smiled. I had a right to be smug. "They got the record deal on their own talent."

His shriek of anger was lost in the wail of guitars.

*

Angrrr Management broke up before they recorded their first album. Some of the members went on to moderate success in other metal bands, although under different names.

As for me, I was lucky enough to escape the 80s without an STD, a drug problem, or another encounter with the Devil.

Well, sort of.

I went back to law school, got my degree. But I went into entertainment law, fighting on the side of the poor stupid artists who, without proper guidance, would sign just about anything to be famous.

WHAT DRAGONS PREFER

I looked down from my horse at the mayor of this town I'd been sent to save, and wondered why I immediately found him so distasteful. Perhaps it was the fact that he had given to titling himself "Lord." Perhaps I was picking up clues from the townsfolk, particularly the women, who avoided him even as they crowded around me.

Or perhaps it was the way his eyes slid over me as he tried to see exactly what lay beneath my leather jerkin.

"Dragonslayer," he greeted, his smile slick beneath his well-oiled mustache. "Thank you for coming to aid us in our time of terror."

"I prefer 'Dragonseeker,'" I said politely. "It is not enough to have the skills to slay a dragon—one must learn about him as well. To know one's enemy is to destroy him."

And most people knew so little about dragons. I knew, for example, that dragons only fed once every twenty years, and then usually only one human. Is that such a bad thing, really, when wolves kill so many deer in the forest to survive, or humans kill sheep because roast mutton is so tasty? But people panicked if they saw a dragon glide far overhead on the highest currents, or if they caught a faint whiff of its acrid scent when the wind turned just right.

He insisted I spend the night in comfort at his home. I found something else to dislike: his manor was too opulent compared to the rest of the farming village, and had been built, no doubt, at the townsfolk's expense. It even had a rooftop garden!

"Do you lure the dragons with your virginity?" he asked during dinner.

"No," I said. I suspected he was less interested in how I lure dragons than in my possible virginal state. My supposition was confirmed when he muttered, "Pity," and turned his attentions to his meal.

I bolted the door to my room that night, and a good thing, for the latch rattled and I heard a thwarted curse.

*

I arose the next morning before dawn and before the mayor, whom I doubted had seen a sunrise in many a year. I, on the other hand, knew that dragons are nocturnal, and would find this one sleeping when I reached its lair.

While I hastily ate a cold sausage roll and drank a cup of tea standing up in the kitchen, I asked his cook if the dragon had carried off many of the town's residents.

"Hardly likely," she snorted, slapping her fists into the bread dough. "His lordship makes sure each girl is 'protected,' as he says, barely a day past their first blooding."

The tea turned bitter on my tongue. So he thought ridding the town's young girls of their virginity would keep the dragon at bay? My instincts about him had been all too correct.

I rode off to find the dragon.

*

"All that's left is discussion of my payment," I told him when I returned the next evening. When I suggested we hold the discussion in his rooftop garden, his smile grew far too broad.

I had barely tucked the purse in my belt and dodged his first advance when the dragon arrived for her twenty-year meal.

Another thing few people know about dragons is that while the males prefer female virgins, the females like their men experienced.

Know your enemies, indeed.

Publication Information

"Accidental Victim" originally appeared in *Vermont Voices II*, League of Vermont Writers, 1994.

"Creative Arsenal" originally appeared in *Jackhammer* e-zine, 2000.

"The Devil Went Down to the Sunset Strip" originally appeared in *Retro Spec: Tales of Fantasy and Nostalgia*, Raven Electrik Ink, 2010.

"A Matter of Perspective" originally appeared in *Scheherezade*, 2004.

"The Power to Change the Shape of the Land" originally appeared in *Sword & Sorceress XVI*, 1999, and was reprinted in *Breaking Waves: An Anthology for Gulf Coast Relief*, Book View Café, 2010.

"The Pumpkin-Carving Contest" originally appeared in *Crossed Genres*, 2014.

"Return" originally appeared in *Raven Electrick*, 2002.

"The Sultan's Sons" originally appeared in *Clash of Steel: Assassin*, Carnifex Press, 2005

"What Dragons Prefer" originally appeared in *Marion Zimmer Bradley's Fantasy Magazine*, 1994, and was reprinted in *Dragons: A Celebration of the Greatest Mythological Creatures*, Starlance Publications, 1996.

About the Author

DAYLE A. DERMATIS has been called "one of the best writers working today" by *USA Today* bestselling author Dean Wesley Smith. Under various pseudonyms (and sometimes with coauthors), she's sold several novels and more than a hundred short stories in multiple genres. A recent transplant to the lush climate of Oregon, in her spare time she follows Styx around the country and travels the world, all of which inspires her writing. She loves music, cats, Wales, TV, magic, laughter, and defying expectations. To find out where she is today, check out www.DayleDermatis.com.